every fig has a wasp inside

Tian Sanchez-Ballado

Select poems may appear in revised form elsewhere, with acknowledgment of first publication where applicable.

ISBN: 979-8-9990663-3-6

Cover artwork and design by Tian Sanchez-Ballado

First edition printed in Tallahassee, Florida

for what survived

for what softened

for what remained sweet

I am out with lanterns, looking for myself.
— Emily Dickinson, in a letter to Mrs. Mary Bowles, 1865

Before You Begin
This collection includes references to sexual violence, emotional and physical abuse, disordered eating, and complex family trauma.

I offer this note not as a warning, but as a lantern. If you need to look away, close the book, or turn the page—do.

You know your own timing.
Thank you for meeting me in mine.

Table of Contents

IV. What Dissolves, Sweetens

V. Wings, Torn but Beautiful

I. Smaller Than My Body

Despite
(after the voicemail I still haven't deleted)

I changed my number.
Not in anger—
after offering every door
and watching you choose
the wall.

Seven months, two weeks, four days.
Not that I'm counting.
You have my husband's number,
my email—everything you need.

The voicemail before the silence:
your voice still calling me by my nickname,
still bright with the assumption
I would always answer.
Before you learned I meant it
when I said enough.

Sometimes I listen to it.
Not often.
Just when I forget
the exact pitch
of how you sound
when you love me.

the difference between
loving someone

and holding your breath.

The love exists.
Not pure. Not hopeful.
Just factual. Just there.
Like muscle memory.
Like my handwriting.
Like the space
where a tooth was.

I practice not waiting.
Practice the ordinary cruelty
of continuing.
Coffee in the morning.
Dinner at seven.
Dreams where you still
know who I am.

Your coordinates rest
in my husband's phone.
Unused.
Like a light left on
in an empty house—
not for hope,
just forgetting
to turn it off.

Hypochondriac

I.   *Collapse*

my dad collapsed
on the bedroom tile—
white, with icy blue veins
like something under skin.

one of the paramedics
was in a rock band with him.
he sang.

at the hospital,
he coded.
twice.

afterwards,
he said an angel told him
to stop and smell the roses.
they called it grace.

when i said
my hands locked,
my body fuzzed out like static—
they said probably anxious.

i puked gushers
all over the leather seats—
red apple yankee candle
sweet and choking.

that's when she believed me.
when the damage
was visible.

II. *Professor*

my professor told me
i was a people pleaser
like diagnosis—
like she'd cracked my code.

the day my hands shook, she said:
you're overthinking. just do it.

the day i forgot a passage i'd played since seventeen:
maybe this isn't the right path for you.

when my spine
started fusing shut,
she handed me Neff
like a prescription.

do you need me to be more nurturing?
the trap.
say yes: prove you're a pig.
say no: consent to the abuse.

she bought me lattes after.
four dollars
to sweeten cruelty.

i have her voice
in my phone
where the poison lives.

III. *Diagnosis*

someone listened.
finally.

a doctor who said: *it's not in your head. it's in your blood.*

Too Afraid

(for the parts of me you clapped for while I died)

that night,
i ate without math.
just stood at the fridge
and didn't measure—
spooned frosting from the tub,
ate cereal from the box
like it might spell my name.

nothing holy.
just a boy
too afraid to be hungry
& too ashamed to stop.

in the morning:
five miles.
then the bowl.
white as a hospital.
quiet as guilt
trying not to echo.

i knelt.
tile pressed its cold into me
like it knew.
i gagged.
just air.
just the ache pretending to be enough.

broth.
so i wouldn't faint.
toothpaste.
so no one would smell it.
mirror:
check if i still deserved
to be seen.

i practiced my wellness in public.
greens.
gratitude.
a hoodie big enough to hide my ribs.

at home,
i stripped.
stepped on glass.
waited for the numbers
to name me good.

until the hunger
became discipline,
the ache
became prayer,
and the vanishing
became the only thing
they ever saw in me—

not the bleeding,
not the boy destroyed,
just the incredible shrinking thing

they could measure
and envy
and watch
disappear.

I Brought a Dead Animal to School

The cool kids had Lunchables—
plastic rectangles of playground power.
Sweaty pepperoni.
Rubber cheddar.
A Capri Sun if your parents really loved you.
You could trade them like cigarettes in prison.

I tried once.
Got laughed at for offering
a pastelito wrapped in napkin,
flaky dough bleeding guava
like an open wound.

The next day,
I came back with a Country Crock tub—
label half-faded,
reeking of home.

Cuban crackers—thick, crumbling.
Cream cheese.
Guava paste, sticky and musky.
Strawberry candies I've never seen in stores,
hidden in the pantry of a house
that smelled like Suavitel
and purple Fabuloso.

I didn't know I was doing it—
bringing a dead animal to school.
That's what one boy whispered
when he saw the raisins,
the olives,
the bay leaf
in my mom's picadillo.

"What is it?"
"Armadillo?!"

The circle widened.
Six feet.
Then ten.

Like I was contagious.
Like being Cuban
could spread.

I ate standing up
in the corner by the trash cans,
trying to make myself smaller
with each bite.
Tasted salt—
food or tears,
I couldn't tell.

I begged for Lunchables.
Got on my knees
in the Publix aisle.

Made promises:
I'd practice piano more.
I'd clean my room.
I'd stop being difficult.
I'd stop being different.
I'd stop.

My mother's face—
I can still see it.
Not disappointment.
Grief.

Like I was asking her
to erase herself
for $4.29.

Eventually, they gave in.
One Lunchable.
Pizza kind.
For Fridays only.

A special treat
that cost more than they said.

I carried it to school
like a trophy.
Like proof I belonged.
Saved it all week,
watching others eat theirs—
casual, careless—

while I counted days.
Friday came.
I opened it at the lunch table
like communion.
Like salvation.
Bit into processed cheese
and waited to transform.

Tasted nothing.
Beige.
Absence.
The flavor of assimilation—
which is no flavor at all.

And I knew
I'd begged my parents
to buy me nothing.
To spend money we didn't have
on emptiness.

So Monday came back
with the Country Crock,
the Goya can,
the chip clip,
the vengeance.

But they'd already won.
I'd already learned
to hate what fed me.

By sixth grade,
I had the system down:
Unwrap in silence.
Chew invisible.
Swallow shame.
Fold the evidence
into the smallest possible square.
Throw it away
before anyone could see.

Speed-eating in bathroom stalls.
The echo of shame
off porcelain and tile.
The taste of home
mixed with the smell
of industrial disinfectant.

Twenty years later,
I still eat too fast.
Still check who's watching.
Still feel six feet of space
around every meal
that smells like memory.

My husband says the food
tastes like love.
I nod.
I smile.
I don't tell him
it tastes like survival.

Like swallowing myself
one spoonful at a time.

II. Blooming Inward

Six Salts

9:30 AM. Pills first.
Monday through Sunday
lined up, AM/PM
written in Sharpie
so I don't forget
which ones
keep me upright.

abuela's cafetera
waits on the stove—
aluminum octagon,
older than my mother,
blackened at the base
from decades of ritual.

But today: cold brew
from the gallon jug.
Lucky Goat roast
over ice
while I count:

Six salts—
Diamond Crystal,
iodized,
Maldon,
smoked,
black salt for dal I keep meaning to make,
pink Himalayan

because someone said
minerals.

Goya beside the $40 olive oil.
Sazón sharing shelf space
with Kashmiri chili—
that jar of hing sealed twice
so it doesn't haunt.

The freezer holds
fifteen Uncrustables.
Sometimes I eat them frozen
when the Pristiq hits
and I'm eight years old again,
crunching salted peanut butter
like stolen joy.

From freezer to counter:
Rice cooker (daily),
Vietnamese coffee maker—
when I'm homesick
for a home I've never seen—
Nespresso for mornings
sleep couldn't reach.

The good moka pots
live on abuela's dresser—
now our sideboard,
dark wood holding
her coffee makers

next to our teapots and tchotchkes,
eclectic, warm,
nothing she'd recognize
but she'd probably love.

No window here.
Dark cabinets.
Everything I own
that matters
fits in this shadowed inventory:
what keeps me alive
(Leflunomide, Zoloft),
what keeps me Cuban
(guava paste, the cafetera),
what keeps me trying:
six kinds of salt
for a life with flavor.

Sunday morning:
I take my pills,
drink cold coffee,
eat rye from the farmer's market
while my husband sips Nespresso.
The bananas go brown.
The rice cooker sings.
Everything necessary
and nothing simple
in this kitchen
where I practice
staying alive.

Before Coffee

He's already out there—
deep squat by the orchids,
heels flat, hands clasped
behind his back like a man
with nowhere else to be.

One finger tests a leaf.
The diagnosis takes
thirty seconds. He shifts
the pot two degrees.
The light agrees.

I'm supposed to be
making coffee. Instead
I'm standing at the balcony door
watching him find
the new spike—

his whole body lifts,
that small bounce
when the world
surprises him
with something good.

Rosemary: quarter turn.
Aster: two inches left.
Goldenrod: perfect.
His hands know things
mine don't.

When he comes in
I'm at the counter,
pouring cold brew
over ice like I've been
here all along.

He smells like morning
and tomorrow's rain.
Tells me about the spike.

Yeah? I say,
ice cracking in the glass—
my hands steady as if
I haven't been standing
at the door this whole time,
memorizing him.

The Last Cafecito
(for abuela, and whoever comes next)

The first time I made it for her,
I was nine. Maybe ten.
Standing on tiptoes at the stove.
Her whole face changed—
told the neighbors, the Castellanos
(whom… she didn't always like):
He made it himself.
Drank it slower than usual.
Like I'd handed her
a piece of her own homeland
she hadn't seen in decades—
still warm.

She made it the old way:
with milk, enough sugar
to make the sugar cane fields blush,
and cornflakes poured right in—
yellow 1960s mug, chipped lip.
Always from memory.
No measurements, just feel.

On Sundays, she'd wait
until the whole house stilled.
Brew it in the background
while telenovelas played reruns.
Even when the cafetera whined,
needed a new gasket,

or caught on the burner—
she kept it.
Cleaned it.
Said it still worked,
and so would she.

She used to say
the smell helped her think.
Even on days
thinking hurt.

She didn't teach me how.
I watched.
Learned the click
when the seal's just right,
the sound of the flame,
the little hiss
before the rise.

She's gone now.
But I still make it.
In her pot.
The aluminum blackened
at the base from decades
of the same ritual.
I don't clean it too much.
Some things deserve
to stay seasoned.

My husband doesn't drink it often.
But he loves the smell.
My mother-in-law asks for it
every visit—calls it cafecito,
says it tastes like coming home
to a place she never lived.

When I'm sick, I make it.
When I'm scared,
grieving,
trying,
I make it.
Not for the caffeine.
For the remembering.

I add a pinch of salt
to the grounds now—
something my abuelo did.
I don't know why.
I just do.

One day, I'll pass it down.
That pot. That scent.
That act of staying
when everything else goes.
I don't think I'll need a recipe.
I never had one.

It's just
what you do

with what you were given—
bitter or sweet.

Strawberry Banana God Particle
(Walter Take the Wheel)

Whole Foods. I ask Kayleigh where the plátanos are.

She lights up.
"Ooh! Frozen?"

Already walking—
ponytail bouncing
like she's leading a meditation
sponsored by yogurt.

We pass probiotic endcaps,
lavender soap wrapped in butcher paper,
a child asking if kale is a feeling.

She stops at a freezer.
Opens it like it's a gift.

"Here they are!"

Strawberry. Banana. Fruit. Blend. Pink and beige bag.
Organic. Good Source of Fiber— printed like a verdict.

Strawberries mid-leap,
bananas in tasteful rotation,
arranged like they're auditioning
for a dental office mural.

No people.
No place.
Just fruit
in the void.

She smiles
like she's done something holy.
Like she's standing
aboard the USS Abraham Lincoln—
a MISSION ACCOMPLISHED banner
made of frozen produce.

I smile back
like I deserved
this kind of rescue.

I don't say:
That's not what I meant.
That's not what I asked for.
That's not even food.

I nod.
And we stand there—
two people
staring into a bag
that says nothing
and means everything.

I'm wearing my Walter Mercado shirt.
A woman says:

"I love your shirt!"

I don't ask
if she knows who he is,
or just thinks
he looks funny—
another brown thing
made safe by camp,
another prophet
turned punchline.

I say thanks.
Again.
Always thanks.

We buy cake instead. Berry chantilly. Strawberries sunk
in cream. We eat it in the car. A plastic container we
pass between us like a kind of surrender— sugar to fill
the space where *plátanos* should be.

At home, I Google: difference between *plátano and
plantain* even though I know.

I'm not looking for fruit.
I'm looking for proof
that there's a difference
between what I asked for
and what I received.

Walter, I asked for *plátanos*. She gave me strawberry banana. Someone loved your shirt but maybe meant your costume. I ate cake in a parking lot to wash down the nothing.

I said thank you.
Three times today.
For things that erase me.

Mucho, mucho, amor.
But even that sounds like begging for translation.

We Call It Sweet

My friend holds my book like a bird that might dissolve.
The cover: dark purple,
a wasp suspended
in amber light. *Every fig*, she starts—
but I'm already moving.

3pm. My hands know this:
the weight of fruit, the way
a knife finds the soft spot.

She watches me quarter the fig—
my fingers long like his were,
trembling like his did,
like mine always have.
Inheritance is a medical condition.

The laugh breaks from me—
too loud, eating all the air,
my abuelo's laugh exactly.
Not similar. Exactly.
Even my joy is haunted.

She shifts on one foot,
thumb grazing the rim of her coffee.
She doesn't ask the question,
but I see it hanging off her wrist
like a charm that meant something once.

Now, let me ask you a question,
I hear myself say,
my mother's voice
stealing my mouth—
You want some?

The fridge hums its one note.
Birds I can't see sing
through walls. This kitchen
has no windows, but watch:
I make the light myself.

Mango, slippery
as memory, staining
everything it touches.

Then strawberry. Too red.
Too easy. Too much like
something Whole Foods would freeze
and call ancestral.
Not all fruit is welcome here.
Some sweetness is a lie.

Each fruit a generation:
fig for the grandfather
who laughed too loud,
pineapple for the mother
who questions everything,
mango for the me
still learning to swallow.

She sets the book down,
pages spread on granite.
Still waiting
for an explanation.

Instead, I spoon honey yogurt
into a bowl, add granola,
nestle the fruit
like small gems.

This is the answer:
We dress death in honey.
We make it Thursday snack.
We eat it with hands
that shake, voices that break
into other people's joy.

I bite through skin
to the seeds beneath—
each one a wasp,
a wing torn off for sweetness,
a body made fruit
by the simple fact
of being devoured.

My friend takes the bowl
I offer. We stand
at the dark granite counter,
barefoot, consuming
what consumed itself
to feed us.

This is what we do
with the bodies:
We call it *sweet*.

III. Bodies Becoming Fruit

Florida Man

I. Before Pulse Was Pulse

My friends drove me
twenty-five minutes
to a club
where I could breathe.

It was just Tuesday.

Later, I did the math—
how many Tuesdays
I missed by inches.

A friend texted:
thank God you weren't there.

I didn't answer.
I knew their names.

II. *Faculty Meeting*

They hand us scanners.
Every ISBN.
Every shelf.

Someone whispers:
Are they taking *Handmaid's Tale?*
Another: *Beloved?*
Two Boys Kissing?

We scan our classrooms
like crime scenes.

Izzie asks
if they'll take her favorite book.

I say,
It's just counting.

She knows
counting comes first.

III. *Teaching While*

Not closeted.
Careful.

Some words
send parents
to the principal.

Some photos
stay off the desk.
Spouse becomes
a shrug.

The day they banned pronouns,
Izzie asked why.

I said,
some people…

She said,
but not you.

And I lied.

IV. Reasons to Stay

Because the bottle missed.

Because drowning here
at least I know
the name of the water.

Because leaving
feels like letting them win.

Because my husband
still holds the mailbox
like it might hold
something worth staying for.

Because Izzie deserves
more than your
funeral prayers
for a state
still breathing.

V. Florida Man

We're still here—
registering voters
in parking lots,
replacing signs
before sunrise,
writing back
when the letters come
spelled wrong.

You call us
lost.
Gone.
Too far.

That's easier than saying
you left.

This is what remains
when the water rises
and doesn't leave.

We stay.
We name the flood.
We remember everything.

We hold on anyway.

The People Who Text You "Are You Alive?" When it Matters
(for the ones who didn't wait for a performance)

They send the video anyway— him screaming the *Bluey*
theme, shirt half-on, juice box in hand. No caption.
Just: *we thought of you.*

They remember I'm an only child
and still invite us to birthdays.
Because we're uncles.
Because they said so.

They clock the hat indoors.
The skipped dinner.
The greased-back hair.

They don't say
"Want to talk about it?"

They say,
"Khachapuri's hot—
 we'll talk about your parents,
mine too."

They don't post about it.
They don't spiritualize it.

They just say:
"Eat this first."

No talk of resilience.
No performance of grace.
Just the way someone
does your dishes
without asking
why you didn't.

And that's it.
That's the whole reason
I'm still here.

Ouija Boards, Crunchy Peanut Butter, and Other Magic

After soccer at Academy of the Holy Names, we piled
into the car— sweaty shin guards, grass-stained socks,
TLC singing *Waterfalls*, rice cakes with crunchy peanut
butter, and grapes so cold they shocked your teeth into
believing again.

We weren't allowed
to read at the kitchen table.
So we did.

Sick, again—
the boy with the hole in his ear.
He's like you, they said.
And I didn't flinch.

Let me bedazzle
my Levi's jacket
with stick-on rhinestones,
leave chalk spells in the garage,
learn which names we never erased

I found the Ouija board
in the cabinet once—
but they nudged me toward Uno
and smiled
like that was magic enough.

They let me sit
with the big kids—
cross-legged on concrete,
listening, watching.

AJ in black.
Camille with the eyeliner
and the perfect eye roll.
Friends in oversized tees
and voices like tambourines.

I didn't know the word yet,
but I knew the rhythm.

I wanted their magic.
Their ease.
The way they worked
at Banana Republic and Gap,
folding denim like ritual,
changing the climate

The piano in the living room
became their hands.
Each note
a kind of holding.

They never told me to be less boy. Or more. They just
passed the glue gun, said *again, but sparklier.*

They made space—

at the chalkboard,
at the table,
at the edge of the patio
with the big kids—
some like me
(but I didn't yet know how).
Sisters I didn't have words for.
Safety I mistook
for magic at first.

I followed them—
to puzzles,
to Limewire,
to a future
they already saw in me.

They never said it.
They didn't need to.
They just loved louder than the questions.

The Fruity Group
(for AT, AS, GM, JG, KW, LY, SW, and wherever the fuck TV landed internationally today)

Thursday. 3:07 PM face is leaking again
either sinuses or the rapture leaning rapture

"at least yours isn't CHUNKY"
"that's blood btw"
"anyway, target has shorts on sale"

(flowchart drops:)
→ mercury in retrograde
→ polyester crimes
→ gay allergies (circled twice)
→ that man from tuesday
→ god's personal vendetta

sips Capri Sun
"hydrate, whore."
"that's my therapist."
(we heart react without irony)

(video arrives:)
baby laughs → panics
caption: "staff meeting energy"
we all type "same"
at the same time.

(reappears after 132 days of silence) "tell them you're crying about your lactose intolerance" (but seriously don't shit yourself there) *(leaves again. we heart react. we continue.)*

(voice memo starts:)
"okay so, gay people and histamines—"
"it's homophobia, brenda"

(photo: mid-slide, mid-dirt, mid-glory)
"this is my Met Gala"
"you're bleeding"
"it's called commitment"

(voice memo from the musical theater faction:)
"TELL THEM HOW IIIIIII—" (cuts off)
someone sobbing
someone singing
someone holding hashbrowns like rosary beads

"not the communion wafer"
"ma'am this is a wendy's"
"stop i'm in a parent meeting"
"tell them you're crying about jesus"

Thursday. 8:42 PM someone's baby is in the hospital. we pivot mid-thread— prayers heart reacts meal train links

"which nurse do i fight"
"say the word, i'll drive"

Two days later
"she's discharged!"
i send:
"CONGRATS ON YOUR DISCHARGE"
"BUT SERIOUSLY THANK GOD"

(pause)
"I HATE YOU"
"READ THE ROOM"
"no wait that's perfect"
"promoted to head gay?"

Friday. 2:47 AM (link: fig wasp article)
"we're the wasps, right?"

"dissolving into sweetness."
"that's just teaching public school."
"no it's deeper, babe."

(paragraph arrives:)
symbiosis.
grief with wings.
some things bloom
by mutual unraveling.

"are you out of your mind??"
"yes but also right."

someone's crying about Elphaba
someone's in Amsterdam

someone asks if bruises count as accessories

Saturday. 6:23 AM
love you whores thanks for being my wasps

"shut up."
"no you shut up."
"everyone shut up i'm trying to die."
"mood."
"same."
"same but with better insurance."

the chat never sleeps.
the chat is the wasp.
the chat is the fig.
the chat is the reason
we're still here.
impossibly sweet.

Joy Like a Brick Through A Window

Saturday nursery crawl.

Native Nurseries—
me in a Selena shirt,
trailing my husband
past stokes aster,
compost demo,
strangers debating aphids.

Body = transport.
No middle.
Years lived above
the brainstem.
Years of careful nothing.

Tallahassee Nurseries.
Gardenias like incense.
Windchimes—
the kind that sound
like waking up.

I sit.
Green notebook.
Fat. Safe.
Hand moves
before I say yes.
Not pretty.
Messy—

like throwing up,
but good.

Skin remembers it's skin.
Ribs = not cage.
Blood moves
because it can.

Ten-year-old handwriting returns—
the one that wrote
Star Wars fanfic
to escape the body,
says:
write now.
say it all.

My husband:
"Take your time."
We both know
we'll be back
next weekend.

He sees my face—
new shape.
Sits. Quiet.
Lets me keep going—
car,
lunch,
until it's dry.

107 pages.
I count later.
Shocked.
My body had that much
to say.

He reads it all
in the garden.
"This is it."
"Focaccia?"

Tres leches under oaks.
Salt. Fat. Acid. Heat.
The full taste
I'd forgotten.

Joy after deadness
is not gentle.
Not gradual.
It's a brick
through glass.

Your own aliveness
breaking in,
finding you
on a bench
in suburban Tallahassee,
saying:
Write.
Now.

IV. What Dissolves, Sweetens

Held, This Time
(an answer to the first time)

my first apartment:
no bed,
no candles,
no script.

just you,
me,
and the carpet—
warm from the day,
still holding the sun.

you didn't touch.
you waited.
hands open on your knees—
i'd never seen patience
have a body.

no questions.
no hurry.
one slow kiss
against the floor,
my ribs pressed into carpet,
my breath catching—
then opening.

i didn't flinch.

didn't leave my body.
stayed.
inside my skin,
inside this moment,
inside the warmth
that wanted nothing
but my presence.

after—
3pm, raw daylight.
the migraine hit.
driving to walgreens,
me apologizing
for ruining everything.

you bought excedrin,
dr. pepper,
kissed my temple in aisle three:
"this is everything too."

we showered.
laughed.
water too hot,
both of us pink,
ridiculous,
the headache finally fading
with your hands in my hair.

our indian place—
the booth we always took.

palak paneer,
naan torn by hand,
mango lassi between us.

no furniture at home,
but this table
was ours.

windows down,
driving along water.
your eyes catching light—
brown, amber, gold.
i didn't need words.
the quiet held.

that night,
you fell asleep beside me,
still dressed,
breathing steady—
the first sound
i ever trusted
completely.

this was my real first time.
nothing in me
needed forgiving.
nothing.

Invasive Species
(a love poem for the end of the world)

He walks barefoot into the yard
like he's entering a cathedral.
I follow,
iced coffee,
half-faith.

The grass glistens like a benediction.
He checks the lemon tree.
One fruit.
We cheer.

At the nursery,
he names the leaves—
jasmine, calamansi.
He won't touch the lantana.

"Invasive," he says. "
Kills what was here first."

I nod.
But the riot of it.
The nerve.
How it strangles and blooms
at once.

Past the gardenias,
we pass milkweed,

tanning beds,
Restylane,
two lips beside tulips—
beauty sold by the season.

He picks the healthiest marigolds.

I pretend not to see the ice chest by the register marked
bees — overnight only.

Last night,
a bird hit the window.
This morning,
he waters the blueberries
like they'll fruit anyway.

Maybe we'll plant a fig.
I nod,
brushing soil off his back.

I don't say
that sweetness requires a death.
That every fig
has a body inside.

I watch—
his knees in dirt,
hands full of promise—
and try to believe
in anything

that roots.

What We Grow
(for Arman)

He's the gardener.
Let's not pretend otherwise.
I nod, admire the rosemary,
sniff the milkweed
like I know what I'm looking for.

I've killed every basil we've tried.
But I like watching
what he makes grow:
dill like green lace,
oregano soft and stubborn,
thyme that creeps but never quits.

The lantana tried to come back.
I yanked it before it could flower.
We don't do invasive here.
Not anymore.

There's a bonsai on the shelf—
a gift from my mom to him.
Nothing but branch now.
He keeps watering it.

He sprays neem oil sometimes.
Says it keeps the bad things away.
I believe him.

I'm still learning
how to let something live
without taming it.
How to call this garden mine
even when the hands aren't mine.

More than we take.
Less than we could.
Enough.

You Already Had a Name
(for Rafael Elías Sanchez-Ballado)

I didn't plan to meet you that night.
Not yet.
But there I was—
in some dream space lit
like sunrise through plantation shutters,
a baby in my arms.
You.
Warm. Real. Mine.

Then they came.
Not with thunder.
Not with trumpets.
Just walking.
Three women from three sides
of this life I've built:

abuela Nita,
in her gorgeous white herringbone jacket,
a sundress so bright it felt like blessing;
wearing the same angel pin
the funeral director placed on her
for me.

Grandma Morales,
all sequins and swagger,
white pantsuit she'd wear
on a cruise ship at captain's dinner;

abuelita Herminia,
glowing in white capris and
a flowy blouse,
a single pearl at her neck
catching the light
like she always did when she smiled.

They didn't hover.
They didn't ask.
They knew.

Abuela stepped forward,
touched your head like a prayer,
and said:
Rafael Elías Sanchez-Ballado.

I woke up.
Heart sprinting.
Eyes wet.
Hands still holding
something I hadn't yet earned.

You weren't born.
Not even close.
But your name had arrived.

Like the story tío Ralph told tía Becky:
"Look at the stars.
You and I are going to get married,
and we're going to have two little girls."

Sometimes love knows
before the body catches up.

And when you finally come—
squalling, soft, real—
I'll know the weight of you
the way my hands knew
that morning I woke,
still cradling the space
where you'd been.

V. Wings, Torn but Beautiful

The Pharmacy Tech Knows My Name
(for the pharmacy staff)

She doesn't use
my full name.
Just a nickname—
like we've known each other
for years.
We kind of have.

Same aisle,
same counter,
same cracked barcode reader
taped at the corner.

"How you feeling today?"
she asks,
before I even speak.
Already scanning
the bottle with the right pronouns
and the right dose.

She lines up
the bottles—
Zoloft, Pristiq,
Leflunomide—
like they're groceries,
not confessions.
Shakes the Leflunomide
so I can hear it's full,

turns each label out
so I can read them.

One time,
she caught a mistake
two doctors missed.
Called them.
Waited on hold.
Told me:
"No one's messing this up on my watch."

She never says
"get better."
Never says
"this must be hard."
She just remembers
to bag the omeprazole
separate from the shampoo,
and says
"see you next week,"
like I'm someone
worth coming back for.

Outside,
my husband loads the car.
Inside,
I sign the receipt
with practiced ease.

The pen always runs out,

but they never forget
what I need.

You May Appeal This Decision
PATIENT INTAKE FORM
(ESTABLISHMENT OF CARE)

Pre-existing condition:
☑ EXISTING WHILE HUMAN
Previously denied coverage:
☑ FOR THE CRIME OF NEEDING IT
Emergency contact:
whoever answers at 3am
(insurance company hours: 9–5 EST, closed weekends)

[PRIOR AUTHORIZATION REQUIRED FOR BREATHING]

Have you tried:
☑ yoga
☑ turmeric
☑ just not being sick
☑ dying
(claim denied – death not cost-effective)

Four-hour Inflectra infusion = $8,000
Insurance "allowed amount" = $6,000
Insurance actual payment = $0
(prior auth pending since 2017)

Math: your life < quarterly earnings

[CURRENT SYMPTOMS]
☑ Joints on fire
☑ Stomach dissolving itself
☑ Rage at form letter denials
☑ Fury at "not medically necessary"

☑ Hatred of shareholders
　　　　Who've never counted pills. Never rationed doses.
　　　　Never chosen between medication and meals.

[BILLING TRAUMA ASSESSMENT]
Outstanding balance: $2,476
(for the privilege of staying alive)

Payment plan options:
• Sell plasma
• GoFundMe
• Bankruptcy
• Rich parents?
• Strategic dying

Cost of one month's meds: $3,847
Insurance coverage: "Under review"
Time spent on hold this week: 11 hours
Fucks left to give: 0

[APPEALS HISTORY]
2017: Denied – not severe enough
2018: Denied – too severe
2019: Denied – experimental treatment
　　　　(FDA approved since 2003)
2020: Denied – out of network
　　　　(only specialist within 200 miles)
2021: Partially approved
　　　　(you pay 80%)

[MEDICATION "MANAGEMENT"]
Currently taking:
☑ What insurance suggests won't work
☑ What they'll cover after you fail cheaper options
☑ What they'll deny next quarter

Plus whatever keeps you
from burning down
their corporate headquarters

[PAIN SCALE TRANSLATION]
6 = I can still work to pay your premiums
8 = I'm costing you money
10 = You'd prefer I didn't exist

[PROVIDER NOTES]
Patient presents with:
- Chronic illness
- Acute awareness that CEO makes $21 million
- Inflammatory response to bureaucracy
- Allergic to bullshit

Treatment plan:
Continue fighting for basic care
while insurance counts money
made from denying
what we need
to survive

[CLAIM DENIED]
Reason code 197:
    Being sick is inconvenient to profit margins
You may appeal this decision
Average appeal processing time: your remaining lifespan

Thank you for choosing us
(as if you had a choice)

Sign of the Fish
(storm rolling in)

bags of water,
nailed to the porch—
each with a penny inside.
to keep flies out, they say.

we moved like memory—
cautious, already edited.

he brushed my back. not tenderness. not performative.
just: *i see you. still here.*

by the preserves,
she glanced at me
like a hymn she used to hum.

then to my husband: **"i like your shoes. toe shoes.
like that guy from CSI."**

we laughed— not the high, thin laugh of *please don't hurt
us*, but something lower, realer— the sound of being
seen by someone who knows what it costs to be seen in
spaces like this.

her husband didn't move.
shoulders squared
like a locked door—
but we were on his side of it.

he was keeping
something out,
not us.
the white couples
browsing preserves
had no idea
what had just happened—
how she'd named us
without naming us,
blessed us
without ceremony,
made this white space
survivable
for the time it takes
to buy preserves.

we bent over the jelly jars,
but different now—
spines straighter,
breathing deeper.

passing glances like folded notes from the pulpit—
you're safe with us.

not safe from the space.
not welcome by the walls.
but seen by the only ones
who needed to see.

like a fish drawn in sand.
like a secret handshake
in daylight.

later,
after the old white men left,
we sat on the porch,
storm rolling in.
still here.
breathing easier.

the bag above us trembled,
catching heat,
casting rainbows.

one fly
spun in the light—
 just outside the frame.
but inside something larger—
the protection
of people
who know
what it means
to need protection.

Every Fig Has a Wasp Inside
(fruit born from a body)

The female wasp tears off her wings
to fit through the opening.
She'll never leave.
The fig dissolves her with enzymes,
makes her body fruit.

This is how sweetness works.

I make it at two a.m.
in my abuela's cafetera—
the aluminum one
that outlived her.
Generations of insomniacs
calling it tradition
instead of symptom.

Last night at two a.m.,
I stood at the stove waiting for the hiss
and understood:
this is how we stay awake—
generations of insomniacs
brewing darkness into ritual,
calling it tradition
instead of symptom.

Two Decembers ago, abuelo died.
At his celebration of life,

I played *Ave Maria*.
My bow trembled on the strings—
grief or genetics, I couldn't tell.
Afterward, they touched my face—
his face now,
round behind the same glasses.
They called me by his name.
Again and again.

His name.
Three generations carry it.
Him, gone now.
My father.
Me—
though I go by something else,
something I chose.

His name lives in my legal documents,
starts my signatures,
begins every introduction
I have to correct.

I carry him in my first breath.
Swallow him with every coffee.
See him in every mirror.

My great uncle walked me through his garden
when I was little.
Prize-winning roses.
Yellow ones—

his mother's favorite.
His hands in the soil
gentle as his voice
explaining aphids,
explaining pruning,
explaining patience.
He gave me Yo-Yo Ma CDs.
Told me about seeing Renée Fleming
at the Kennedy Center.
Never married.
Lived thirty years
with his roommate, Tom.

I never told him I was gay.
He never told me.

But he gave me Bach cello suites
and stories about sopranos,
and I think
that was his way of saying
I see you.

Now I plant yellow roses
with my husband.
Our wedding rings catch sunlight—
a sound
my uncle never got to make.

My tía has our abuela's green eyes.
I have them too.

Nobody else.

I wrote a poem once:
we share the same eyes.
Never showed her.

Some recognitions
are too sharp
to speak aloud.
This is what I carry:
My father's cough in my throat each morning.
My abuelo's laugh—
too loud,
taking up all the air,
How I go silent
instead of saying what hurts.

Each time I catch myself,
I think:
Whose voice is this?
Whose hands?
Whose silence?

Mine now.
All of it mine.

My abuela spent days
staring at the ceiling fan.
Now me—
counting rotations

like rosary beads.

In the produce aisle,
I hold each fig to the light.

Inside:
a dissolved wasp—
wings torn off at entry,
body made sugar,
death made sweet.

The wasp must die
for the fig to live.
She thinks she's planting gardens.
She doesn't know
she's being eaten.
The figs in my cart
are heavy with bodies.
I buy them anyway.
Eat them anyway.
Taste the sweetness anyway.

What else can we do
with what we've inherited?

I wake at two a.m.,
make Cuban coffee,
stand at the window
where my father stands,
where his father stood.

The roses need water.

Tomorrow
I'll laugh too loud at nothing.
Tomorrow
I'll catch my mother's tone
in my throat,
my abuela's sadness
in my green eyes,
my family's silence
in my mouth.

Here's what terrifies me:

When I'm angry,
I hear their voices.
When I'm silent,
it's their silence.
When I love,
it's with their same
beautiful
breaking
hands.

I can't tell anymore
where they end
and I begin.
Can't separate
the prize-winning roses
from the hidden love.

The green eyes
from what they saw.
The coffee ritual
from the sleeplessness it serves.
The sweetness
from the dissolution.

I pour the coffee.
Perfect temperature.
Perfect bitterness.
Three a.m. medicine
for an inherited insomnia.

My husband sleeps.
I don't wake him.

This is my inheritance:
learning to swallow darkness
without complaint,
to count ceiling fan rotations
like rosary beads,
to make sweetness
from whatever crawled inside us
to die.
To him.
To her.
To the great uncle who knew without knowing.

The sweetness is real.

Fig Season, Ten Years Later
(for the ones who stayed, and the ones who didn't)

July again.
Figs stacked at the market—
dark, soft,
the color of old bruises.

I bring them home.
Split one open.
Blue cheese.
Salt.
Not pan de higo,
but close enough.

I remember the tree—
the one you planted
because I asked.
The one we left
when it all collapsed.

Fig Newtons in the pantry.
Dad watching TV.
Mom still gentle.
Before everything soured.

Now it's fig jam
on sourdough with butter.
Now I know
what softens,

what ferments,
what survives.

I don't dream
the old life.

What I have is riper.
Stranger.
Better.

I eat slowly.
Feel the seeds crack.
Swallow.
Save what grows.